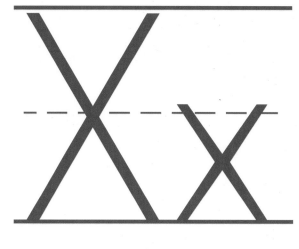

**Warren Rylands
and Samantha Nugent**

LET'S READ

AV² BY WEIGL™

ADDED VALUE • AUDIO VISUAL

Go to **www.av2books.com**, and enter this book's unique code.

BOOK CODE

X987246

AV² by Weigl brings you media enhanced books that support active learning.

AV² provides enriched content that supplements and complements this book. Weigl's AV² books strive to create inspired learning and engage young minds in a total learning experience.

Your AV² Media Enhanced books come alive with...

Audio
Listen to sections of the book read aloud.

Video
Watch informative video clips.

Embedded Weblinks
Gain additional information for research.

Try This!
Complete activities and hands-on experiments.

Key Words
Study vocabulary, and complete a matching word activity.

Quizzes
Test your knowledge.

Slide Show
View images and captions, and prepare a presentation.

... and much, much more!

Published by AV² by Weigl
350 5th Avenue, 59th Floor
New York, NY 10118

Website: www.av2books.com

Library of Congress Control Number: 2015940626

ISBN 978-1-4896-3561-7 (hardcover)
ISBN 978-1-4896-3563-1 (single user eBook)
ISBN 978-1-4896-3564-8 (multi-user eBook)

Printed in the United States of America in Brainerd, Minnesota
1 2 3 4 5 6 7 8 9 0 19 18 17 16 15

052015
WEP050815

Project Coordinator: Katie Gillespie   Art Director: Terry Paulhus

Weigl acknowledges Getty Images and iStock as the primary image suppliers for this title.

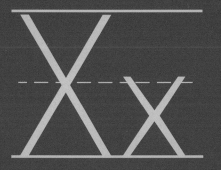

CONTENTS

Let's explore the letter

The uppercase letter X looks like this

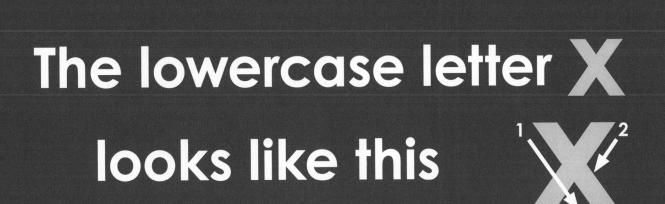

The lowercase letter x looks like this

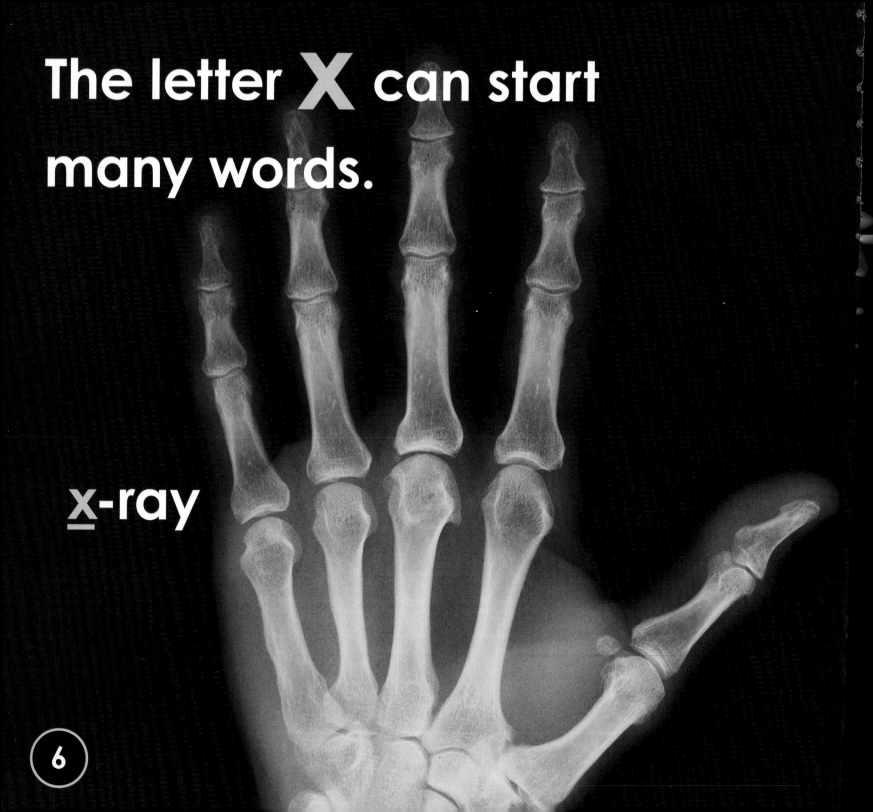

The letter **X** can start many words.

x-ray

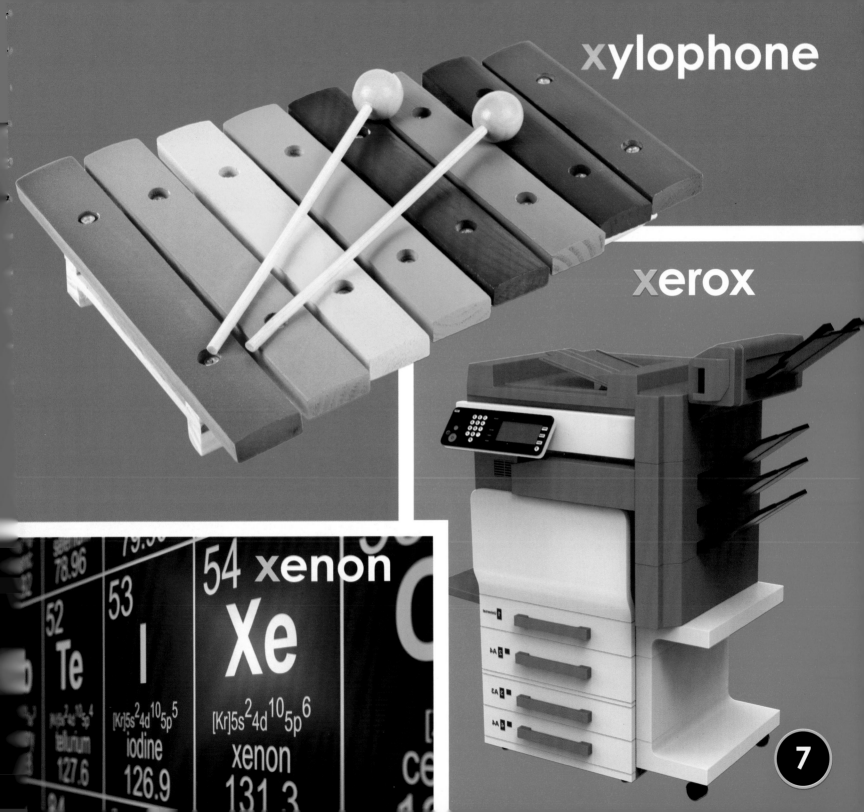

xylophone

xerox

54 xenon

Xe

52
Te
telurium
127.6

53
I
[Kr]5s²4d¹⁰5p⁵
iodine
126.9

54 xenon
Xe
[Kr]5s²4d¹⁰5p⁶
xenon
131.3

78.96

79.90

7

The letter **X** can be inside a word.

boxer

axe

taxi

next

exit

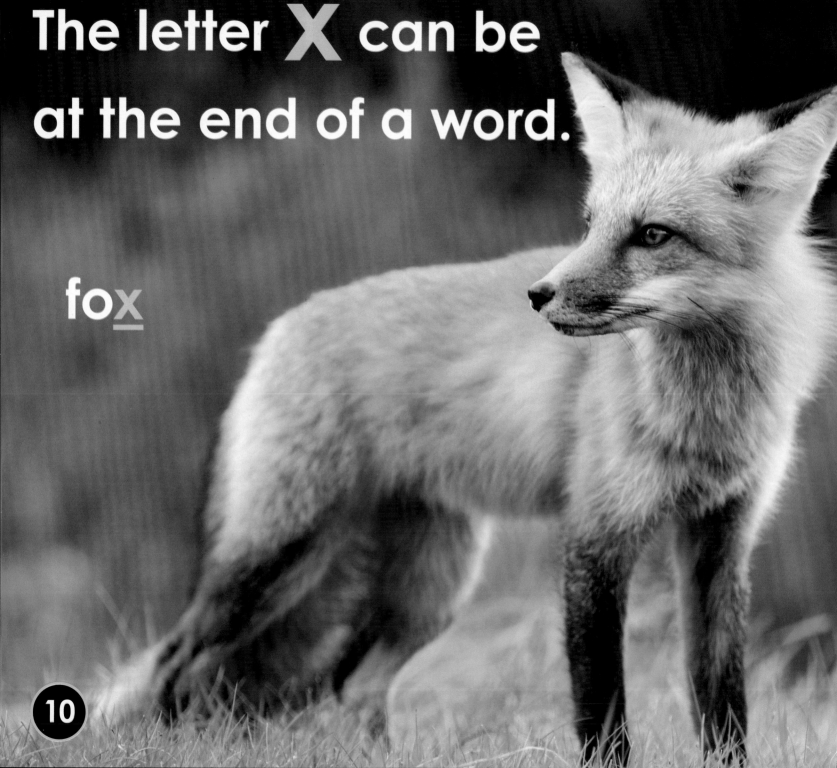

The letter **X** can be at the end of a word.

fo<u>x</u>

lynx

box

wax

fix

11

Many names start with an uppercase X.

Xavi

Xandra loves pizza.

Xavier wears cowboy hats.

Xenia has a red bike.

Xui is a pirate.

13

The letter X makes different sounds.

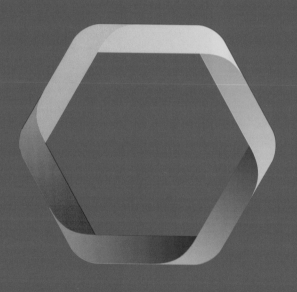

hexagon

six

The letter **X** says its name in the word **hexagon**.

The letter **X** makes a different sound in the word **six**.

The letter **X** can say its name when it comes after the letter e.

flex

extra

explore

excited

explain

Sometimes the letter X sounds like the letters k and s together.

tax

ox

relax

mix

pixie

Having Fun with X

Xavier was excited to explore the city. He took a taxi to the wax museum.

Next, he went to watch the Fox and Ox Band play. Ox played the xylophone very well.

Xavier even had extra time to flex at the gym.

At the end of the day, it was time for Xavier to relax.

The alphabet
has **26** letters.

X is the twenty-fourth
letter in the alphabet.

Aa Bb Cc Dd Ee

Ff Gg Hh Ii Jj Kk

Ll Mm Nn Oo Pp

Qq Rr Ss Tt Uu Vv

Ww **Xx** Yy Zz

23

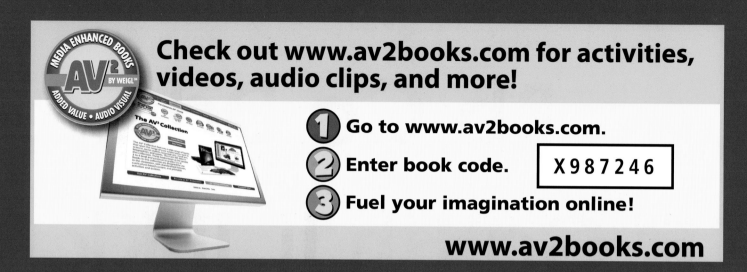